Funky Flamingos

Written by Carol Krueger

Rigby

Flamingos are pink birds.
They live on big lakes.
They have long necks
and long legs.

long neck

long legs

A flamingo can grow
very big for a bird.
Look at the flamingo.
Look at the child.
They are the same size.

feet

4

0

Look at this flamingo.
It has opened its wings.
Now the flamingo
looks bigger!

feet

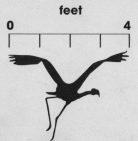

A flamingo has
pink feathers.
Flamingos like to clean
their feathers.

This flamingo is cleaning its feathers. It will clean them for hours and hours every day.

Flamingos like to live
with other flamingos.
Look at how many flamingos
can live in one place!

A million flamingos can live in one place.

A flamingo gets
food with its beak.
It puts its head upside
down in the water.

When its head is in the water, it will not breathe.

A flamingo sucks in
water and food
with its beak.

Look inside
the flamingo's beak.
The beak has bumps.
The food gets stuck
in the bumps.

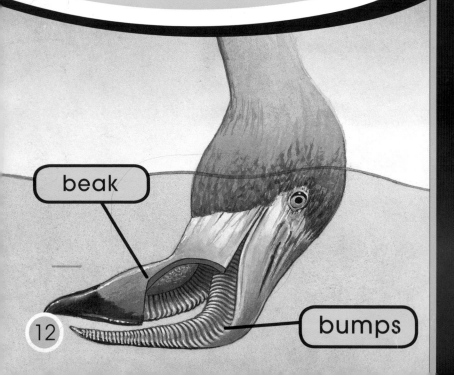

beak

bumps

beak

bumps

The food that flamingos eat makes them pink.
When a flamingo can't eat plants and fish, it goes gray!

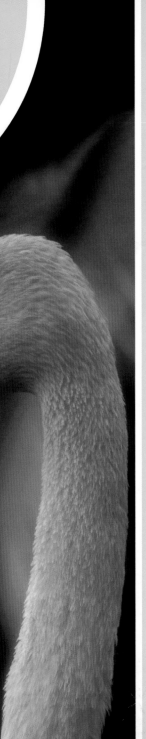

Index

Guide Notes

Title: **Funky Flamingos**
Stage: Early (3) – Blue

Genre: Nonfiction
Approach: Guided Reading
Processes: Thinking Critically, Exploring Language, Processing Information
Written and Visual Focus: Photographs (static images), Index, Labels, Caption, Scale Diagrams
Word Count: 168

THINKING CRITICALLY
(sample questions)
- Look at the front cover and the title. Ask the children what they know about flamingos.
- Look at the title and read it to the children.
- Focus the children's attention on the index. Ask: "What are you going to find out about in this book?"
- If you want to find out about how flamingos eat, which pages would you look on?
- If you want to find out about where flamingos live, which pages would you look on?
- Look at page 7. Why do you think the flamingo cleans its feathers for hours and hours?
- Look at pages 8 and 9. Why do you think so many flamingos live in the same place?

EXPLORING LANGUAGE

Terminology
Title, cover, photographs, author, photographers

Vocabulary
Interest words: flamingo, lake, feathers
High-frequency words: how, many, every, other
Positional words: in, upside down, on, inside
Compound words: upside, inside

Print Conventions
Capital letter for sentence beginnings, periods, commas, exclamation marks